Jacqueline Wilson

BIG DAY OUT

Illustrated by
NICK SHARRATT

CORGI
YEARLING

BIG DAY OUT
A CORGI YEARLING BOOK 978 0 440 86990 0

First published in Great Britain by Corgi Yearling,
an imprint of Random House Children's Books
A Random House Group Company

This edition published 2012

1 3 5 7 9 10 8 6 4 2

'Our Free Day Out' originally published in *The Jacqueline Wilson Summer Annual*,
copyright © Jacqueline Wilson, 2011

'Day Out in the Country' originally published in *More Muck and Magic*
(Egmont), copyright © Jacqueline Wilson, 2001

'Odd One Out' originally published in *Eating Candyfloss Upside Down*
(Puffin), copyright © Jacqueline Wilson, 2003; reprinted in
Totally Jacqueline Wilson (Doubleday, 2007)

'Marty's Big Day Out' copyright © Jacqueline Wilson, 2012

Text copyright © Jacqueline Wilson, 2012
Illustrations copyright © Nick Sharratt, 2012

The Random House Group Limited supports the Forest Stewardship Council (FSC®),
the leading international forest certification organization. Our books carrying the FSC label
are printed on FSC®-certified paper. FSC is the only forest certification scheme endorsed
by the leading environmental organizations, including Greenpeace. Our paper
procurement policy can be found at www.randomhouse.co.uk/environment.

MIX
Paper from
responsible sources
FSC® C016897

Set in 12/16pt New Century Schoolbook

Corgi Yearling Books are published by Random House Children's Books,
61–63 Uxbridge Road, London W5 5SA

www.kidsatrandomhouse.co.uk
www.totallyrandombooks.co.uk
www.randomhouse.co.uk

Addresses for companies within The Random House Group Limited
can be found at: www.randomhouse.co.uk/offices.htm

THE RANDOM HOUSE GROUP Limited Reg. No. 954009

A CIP catalogue record for this book is available from the British Library.

Printed and bound by CPI Group (UK) Ltd, Croydon, CR0 4YY

CONTENTS

Our Free Day Out   1

Day Out in the Country   15

Odd One Out   29

Marty's Big Day Out   49

OUR FREE DAY OUT

Where do you go for your summer holidays? Girls in my class camp in the Lake District or stay on farms in Devon or rent holiday cottages in Cornwall. Some of them go to Spain and come back celebrity brown, with their hair in little beaded braids. Several fly all the way to Florida and boast about braving Space Mountain and have autograph books with Mickey Mouse and Pluto signatures.

We don't ever go on summer holidays. We haven't got any money. There's just Mum and me and the three little ones. Bliss and Baxter are five and little Pixie is two. Pixie has big blue eyes and golden curls and everyone goes 'Aaaah!' when they catch sight of her. Bliss is quite pretty too, though she's so shy she always hangs her head so you can't see her face properly. Baxter looks fierce because of his crew cut but he is kind of cute. People always fuss over them because they're twins. No one ever fusses over me or goes 'Aaaah!' I'm ten, and I'm pale and skinny and I've got a frowny face because I worry a lot.

I was getting especially worried about Mum during the summer holidays because she was so fed up. She just lay on our battered sofa watching the television, not bothering to go out, even when it was sunny. Every time the kids yelled she'd wince and say they were doing her head in. I tried to keep them quiet. I read them stories and we 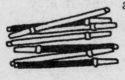 all did drawing together with my felt tips. That wasn't such a good idea, because Baxter drew a

frieze of green monster men all round
the kitchen wall, and Pixie decided to
scribble with Mum's lipstick
instead of a felt pen.

We played pretending
games too. Don't laugh – I know
I'm way too old for that sort of thing,
but it was just to keep the kids happy.
We played we were going to the seaside.
I let the kids strip down to their pants
and splash about in the bath for ages.
They really liked that, but maybe it
wasn't such a good idea either, because
they splashed a bit too much, and the
water seeped through the floorboards
and dripped through the ceiling of
the flat downstairs, and the woman
from number six came up and had a
shouting match with Mum.

'I'm sorry, Mum,' I said miserably.
'We were just pretending we were at
the seaside.'

'Oh, never mind, Lily. She's a right
moany old bag, that one. I know you
didn't mean any harm. I wish I could

take you all to the seaside. I'm going crazy stuck here day after day. It's not doing you lot any good either, cooped up in this little flat.'

We all went out to the launderette together. I helped out doing the washing, Baxter ran around with a plastic basket on his head being a Washing Monster, Bliss looked anxiously at her newly washed teddy spinning round and round in the dryer, and Pixie perched on an old lady's lap and chatted away to her.

'What a little darling!' said the old lady, whose name was Joan. 'But she's so pale. She needs to get some roses in her cheeks.'

'You're telling me,' said Mum. 'But I can't afford to take them anywhere.'

'My church is organizing some free day trips to the seaside – one for mums and kiddies, and the other for all us pensioners. The coaches are leaving from the bus station next Saturday. I think the kiddie special goes at eight o'clock, and I'm sure they've got a few seats left. Your kids could paddle in the sea, build a few sandcastles,  and have fish and chips and ice cream.'

'Oh, wow, Mum!' I said. 'Please say yes. I'd love to paddle in the sea.'

'Fish and chips,' said Baxter, rubbing his tummy.

'Ice cream, ice cream, ice cream!' said Pixie.

'But we don't go to your church, Joan,' said Mum.

'Never mind. I'm on the committee, so I get to say who goes. And I say you lot go, OK?'

'Brilliant,' said Mum.

But it wasn't brilliant at all on Saturday morning. We're not very good at getting up early, especially in the school holidays. Mum set her alarm for seven, but then she slept right through it. I woke up at half past and shot out of bed.

'Oh no, we've slept in. We'll miss the eight o'clock coach!' I said.

'Oh, Lily, shut it. We'll get there in time, you'll see,' said Mum, staggering out of bed.

She got herself and Pixie dressed, while I chivvied Baxter and Bliss into T-shirts and shorts and got dressed myself. There wasn't time for breakfast. Mum gave us a piece of bread and jam to eat on the way, and Pixie sucked at her bottle in the buggy. We ran nearly all the way to the bus station – but it was nearly ten past eight now. We saw the coach disappearing in the distance without us!

'Just my rotten luck!' said Mum, and she looked like she was going to burst into tears.

'Where were you lot then?' said Joan, coming up to us. She was wearing a pink sunhat and a pink flowery dress to match. 'Oh dear, oh dear, don't look so downhearted.'

'But we've missed our chance of a free day at the seaside,' I wailed.

'No you haven't, dearie!' said Joan. 'You lot will simply have to tag along with us old dears instead. Our coach leaves at half past eight. I'm sure there'll be room for you. I can always have little Pixie on my lap.'

So we had our free day out after all! Everybody else on the coach was over seventy. There was one little old man who was ninety-two and in a wheelchair, but Mum and the coach driver, Darren, helped haul him up into the coach. Darren wasn't over seventy – he was about Mum's age, very smiley and jokey, and he got all the old folks singing songs on the journey.

There were plenty of spare seats but Pixie sat on Joan's lap anyway, though she started fidgeting ominously when we were halfway there.

'I think Pixie needs to do a wee!' I said to Mum. 'Can you ask Darren to stop the coach?'

It was absolutely fine, because half the pensioners needed a bathroom break too, so we stopped at this roadside café. Then we were off again, and it wasn't long before we had our first glimpse of the sea. I'd seen it before, of course, but Baxter and Bliss were really thrilled, and Pixie kept yelling, 'Big bath! Big big big bath!' which made everyone laugh.

Darren parked the coach on the promenade and helped everyone down onto the sands. He took off his shirt because it was really warm and sunny. All the old ladies gave him funny wolf-whistles. Darren went as pink as Joan's hat and Mum giggled at him.

I helped Bliss make a great big sandcastle. We decorated it with seaweed and pebbles, and one of the old ladies gave us coloured toffee papers to make stained-glass windows. Baxter kept threatening to jump on it so I made him a separate big castle to demolish. Then he chummed up with an old man and they played football on the beach together. Pixie ran around all the old ladies wearing Joan's sunhat, and they all chuckled and called her a proper caution.

We all went into the sea together for a paddle. Even Darren rolled up his jeans and joined in. The dear old ninety-two-year-old couldn't go in the sea, so Baxter filled two buckets with seawater and he splashed his feet in them instead.

We had fish and chips for lunch, with ice cream for pudding. Pixie's cone fell in the sand, but nearly all the old ladies offered her theirs instead, so she ended up with an

enormous amount of ice cream for one very small girl. I was in charge of Pixie while Mum went for a stroll on the pier with Darren. I kept a careful eye on her in case she was sick, but she didn't disgrace us.

Joan took lots of photos of us on our free day out and she sent us some copies as a souvenir. There's one of Mum, arm in arm with Darren, both of them laughing their heads off. There are heaps of photos of Pixie looking adorable in the pink hat with ice cream all round her face. Baxter and Bliss look great too, playing with their sandcastles. I usually *hate* having my photo taken, but there's one of me grinning right into the camera, my hair blowing back, my forehead not the slightest bit frowny because I'm having such a great time.

We never bumped into the other coach of mums and kids, but it didn't matter a bit. We had a much better time with Joan's friends. I'd still like to have camped in the Lake District or stayed on a farm in Devon or rented a holiday cottage in Cornwall. I'd have absolutely loved to have gone to Spain or Florida. But never mind – I bet I've had the best free day out ever!

If you want to find out more about Lily and Bliss and Baxter and Pixie, then read Jacqueline Wilson's book

DAY OUT IN THE COUNTRY

'**M**ick's coming round on Saturday,' said Mum.

Skippy smiled. She always smiles. If you told her the Bogeyman was coming to take her out to tea she'd clap her hands and smile.

I didn't smile. I can't stick Mick. I don't see why Mum has to have a stupid boyfriend at her age. She says he makes her happy. I can't see why she can't just be happy with Skippy and me.

'Mick's going to take us on a special day out!' Mum announced.

Skippy smiled. I very nearly smiled too. We didn't often get special days out.

I wondered where we might be going. A day trip to Disneyland?!

No, maybe not. But perhaps Mick would take us to the Red River Theme Park and we could go on all the really brilliant rides where you swoop up and down and it's like you're flying right up in the sky.

'Will he take us to the Red River Theme Park, Mum?'

'Don't be daft, Hayley,' said Mum. 'It costs a fortune. Mick's not made of money. No, we're going to have a lovely day out in the country.'

'The *country*?' I said.

'What's the country?' Skippy asked.

'It's boring,' I said.

I hadn't actually been to the country much, but of course I knew all about it. We've got this old video about kids living on a farm in the country. The main girl in it is called Hayley like me. It's a good film but the country looks *awful*. Cold and empty and muddy, with cows that chase you.

I moaned, and Mum said I was a spoiled little whatsit, and I went into our bedroom and sulked. Skippy came and cuddled up beside me.

'We don't like the country,' she said, to show me she was on my side – though Skippy is always on *everyone's* side.

'That's right, Skip. We don't like the country. And we don't like Mick.'

'We don't like Mick,' Skippy echoed obediently, but she didn't sound so sure.

When Mick knocked at our door at nine o'clock on Saturday morning, Skippy went rushing up to him, going, 'Mick, Mick, Mick!'

Skippy is useless at not liking people.

I am brilliant at it. And Mick was making it easy-peasy. He looked *ridiculous*. He always looks a bit wet and weedy, but today he was wearing a big woolly jumper right up to his chin and awful baggy cord trousers and *boots*. Honestly. I knew Mum could act a bit loopy at times but she had to be barking mad to go round with Mick.

'Ready, girls?' he said, swinging Skippy round and round while she squealed and kicked her legs, her shoes falling off. 'Have you got any welly boots, Skip? I think you'll need them.' He put on a silly voice (well, his *own* voice is silly, but this was sillier). 'It gets right mucky in the country, lass.'

Skippy put on my old Kermit wellies and her Minnie Mouse mac.

'It's a Mouse-Frog!' said Mick, and Skippy fell about laughing.

I sighed heavily.

'What about *your* wellies, Hayley?' said Mick. 'And I should put a jumper on too.'

I took no notice. As if I'd be seen dead in wellies! And I was wearing the simply incredible designer T-shirt Mum found for 20p down at the school jumble. I wasn't going to cover it up with an old sweater even if it *snowed*.

Mum looked like she wanted to give me a shake, but she got distracted looking for our old thermos flask. We were having a picnic. I'd helped cut the sandwiches. (Skippy sucked the cut-off crusts until they went all slimy like ice lollies.) The sandwiches were egg and banana and ham (not all together, though maybe it would taste good), and there were apples and crisps and a giant bar of chocolate, and orange juice for Skip and me, and tea for Mum and Mick. It seemed a seriously yummy picnic. It looked like I *might* be going to enjoy this day out in spite of myself.

Skippy and I nagged to nibble the chocolate in the car on the way to the country. Mum said we had to wait till picnic time. Hours and hours and hours! Mick said, 'Oh, let the girls have a piece now if they're really hungry.'

He rooted round in the picnic bag and handed the whole bar over.

This was a serious mistake. Skippy and I tucked in determinedly. By the time Mum peered round at us we'd eaten nearly three-quarters.

Mum was very cross. 'How can you be so greedy? Hayley, you should have stopped Skippy. You know she gets car-sick.'

'She's fine, Mum. Stop fussing. You're OK, aren't you, Skip? You don't feel sick, do you?'

Skippy said she didn't feel sick at all. She tried to smile. She was very pale, though her lips were dark brown with chocolate.

'Oh dear,' said Mum. 'Have you got a spare plastic bag, Mick? We need it kind of urgently.'

She was just in time. Skippy was very very sick. It was so revolting that it made *me* feel a little bit sick too. We drove slowly with the window wide open. I shut my eyes and wondered when we were ever going to get to this boring old countryside. I'd lost interest in the picnic. I just wanted it to be time to go home.

'Here we are,' Mick said cheerily at long long long last.

I opened my eyes and looked round. I hadn't realized the country was going to be so *green*. That old film with the other Hayley was in black and white.

'We used to come here on days out when I was a boy,' Mick said excitedly. 'Isn't it lovely?'

There was nothing much *there*. No shops. No cafés. Not even an ice-cream van. Just lots and lots and lots of trees. And fields. More trees. More fields. And a big big hill in the distance, so tall there were grey clouds all round the top like fuzzy hair.

'That's Lookout Hill,' said Mick. 'Right, girls! Let's climb it!'

I stared at him as if he was mad. Even Mum looked taken aback. He said it as if climbing miles up into the clouds was a big treat! We don't reckon climbing three flights of stairs up to our flat when the lift breaks down.

'Isn't it a bit too far?' said Mum.

'No, no. We'll be up it in a matter of minutes, you'll see,' said Mick.

Mick is a liar. Those few minutes went on for hours. First we trudged through the woods. It was freezing cold and dark and miserable, and I hated it. Mick saw me shivering and offered me his big woolly but I wouldn't wear it. He put it on Skip instead, right over her mac. She staggered along looking loopy, the hem right down round her ankles. Mum said she looked like a little sheep, so Skip went *'Baa-baa-baa.'*

Then we were out of the wood and walking across a field. Skip went skipping about until she stepped in something disgusting. I laughed at her. Then I stepped in something too. I squealed and moaned and wiped my shoes in the grass five hundred times. We seemed to be wading through a vast animal toilet.

'Stop making such a fuss, Hayley. We'll clean your shoes properly when we get home,' said Mum.

She didn't look as if she was enjoying the country that much either. Her hair was blowing all over the place and her eye make-up was running.

'Now for the final stretch,' said Mick, taking Mum's hand. She held onto Skippy with the other.

I hung back. I climbed up after them. Up and up and up and up. And up and up and up. And up some more.

My head hurt and my chest was tight and a stitch stabbed my side and my legs ached so much I couldn't keep up.

'This sucks,' I gasped, and I sat down hard on the damp mucky grass.

'Come on, Hayley!' Mick called, holding out his other hand.

'No thanks. I'll wait here. I don't want to go up the stupid hill,' I said.

'You've got to come too, Hayley,' said Mum. 'We can't leave you here by yourself.'

So they forced me up and I had to stagger onwards. Up and up and up and up. I wasn't cold any more. I was boiling hot. My designer T-shirt was sticking to me. My shoes were not only all mucky and spoiled, but they were giving me blisters. If I was as little as Skippy I might have started crying.

'It'll be worth it when we get right to the top and you see the view,' said Mick.

What view? He was crazy. We were right up in the clouds and it was grey and gloomy and drizzling.

'Nearly there!' Mad Mick yelled above me. 'See!'

Then Mum gasped. Skippy squeaked. And I staggered up after them out of the clouds – and there I was on the top of the hill and the sun was suddenly out, shining just for us, right above the clouds in this private secret world in the air. There were real sheep munching grass and a Skippy-sheep capering round like crazy. I stood still, my heart thumping, the breeze cool on my hot cheeks, looking up at the vast sky. I saw a bird flying way up even higher. I felt as if I could fly too. Just one more step and I'd be soaring.

The clouds below were drifting and parting, and suddenly I could see the view. I could see for miles and miles and miles – the green slopes and the dark woods and the silver river glittering in the sunlight. I was on top of the whole world!

'Wow,' I said.

Skippy smiled. Mum smiled. Mick smiled. And I smiled too. Then we all ran hand in hand down down down the hill, ready for our picnic.

ODD ONE OUT

I'm the odd one out in the family. There are a lot of us. OK, here goes. There's my mum and my stepdad Graham and my big brother Mark and my big sister Ginnie and my little sister Jess and my big stepbrother Jon and my big stepsister Alice, and then there's my little half-sister Cherry and my baby half-brother Rupert. And me, Laura. Not to mention my real dad's new baby and his girlfriend Gina's twins, but they live in Cornwall now so I only see them for holidays. Long holidays, like summer and sometimes Christmas and Easter. Not short bank holidays, like today.

It's a bank holiday and that means an Outing.

I hate Outings. I like Innings. My idea of bliss would be to read my book in bed with a packet of Pop Tarts for breakfast, get up late and draw or colour or write stories, have bacon sandwiches and crisps and a big cream cake or two for lunch, read all afternoon, have a whole chocolate Swiss roll for tea in front of the telly, draw or colour or write more stories, and then pizza for supper.

I've never enjoyed a day like that. It wouldn't work anyway because there are far too many of us if we all stay indoors, and the big ones hog the sofa and the comfy chairs, and the little ones are always dashing around and yelling and grabbing my felt tips. And Mum is always trying to stop me eating all the food I like best, pretending that a plate of lettuce and carrots and celery is just as yummy as pizza(!), and Graham is always suggesting I might like to get on this bike he bought me and go for a ride.

I wish he'd get on *his* bike. And take the whole family with him. And most of mine. Imagine if it was just Mum and me . . .

We had to do a piece of auto-biographical writing at school last week on 'My Family'. I pondered for a bit. Just writing down the *names* of my family would take up half the page. I wanted to write a proper story, not an autobiographical list. So I had an imaginary cull of my entire family apart from Mum, and wrote about our life together as a teeny-weeny two-people family. I went into painstaking detail, writing about birthdays and Christmas and how my mum sometimes produced presents that had *Love from Daddy* or *Best Wishes from Auntie Kylie in Australia* – although I knew she'd really bought them herself. I even pretended that Mum sometimes played at being my gran or even grandpa and I played at being her son or her little baby. I wrote that although we played these games it was just for fun. We weren't lonely at all. We positively *loved* being such a small family.

Mrs Mann positively loved my effort too! This was a surprise because Mrs Mann is very, very strict. She's the oldest teacher at school and she can be really scary and sarcastic. You can't mess around in Mrs Mann's class. She wears these neat grey suits that match her grey hair, and white blouses with tidily tied bows, and a pearl brooch precisely centred on her lapel. You can tell just by looking at her that she's a stickler for punctuation and spelling and paragraphing and all those other boring, boring, boring things that stop you getting on with the story. My piece had its fair share of mistakes ringed in Mrs Mann's red rollerball, but she *still* gave me a ten out of ten because she said it was such a vivid, truthful piece of heartfelt writing.

I felt a little fidgety about this. Vivid it might be, but truthful it *isn't*. When Mrs Mann was talking about my small family, my friends Amy and Kate stared at me open-mouthed because I'm always whining on to them about my *big* family. Luckily they're not tell-tales.

Sometimes I get on better with all my Steps. My big stepbrother Jon likes art too, and he always says sweet things about my drawings. My big stepsister Alice isn't bad either. One day when we were all bored she did my hair in these cool little plaits with beads and ribbons, and made up my face so I looked almost grown up. Yes, I like Jon and Alice, but they're much older than me so they don't really want me hanging out with them.

The Halfies aren't bad either. I

quite like sitting Cherry on my lap and reading her *Where the Wild Things Are*. She always squeals when I roar their terrible roars right in her ear and Mum gets cross, but Cherry *likes* it. Rupert isn't into books yet – in fact I was a bit miffed when I showed him my old nursery-rhyme book and he *bit* it, like he thought it was a big bright sandwich. He's not really fun to play with yet because he's too little.

That's the trouble. Mark and Ginnie and Jon and Alice are too big. Jess and Cherry and Rupert are too little. I'm the Piggy in the Middle.

Hmm. My unpleasant brother Mark frequently makes grunting snorty noises at me and calls me Fatty Pigling.

I have highly inventive nicknames for Mark – indeed, for *all* my family (apart from Mum) – but I'd better not write them down or you'll be shocked.

I said a few very rude words to myself when Mum and Graham said we were going for a l-o-n-g walk along the river for our bank holiday outing. It's OK for Rupert. He goes in the buggy. It's OK for Cherry and Jess. They get piggyback rides the minute they start whining. It's OK for Mark and Ginnie and Jon and Alice. They stride ahead in a little gang (or lag behind, whatever), and they talk about music and football and s-e-x, and whenever I edge up to them they say, 'Push off, Pigling,' if they're Mark or Ginnie, or, 'Hi, Laura, off you go now,' if they're Jon or Alice.

I'd love it if it could just be Mum and me going on a walk together. But Graham is always around and he makes silly jokes or slaps me on the back or bosses me about. Sometimes I get really narked and tell him he's not my dad so he can't tell me what to do. Other times I just *look* at him. Looks can be very effective.

My face was contorted in a *dark scowl* all the long, long, long trudge along the river. It was so incredibly boring. I am past the age of going 'Duck duck

duck' whenever a bird with wings flies
past. I am not yet of the age to collapse
into giggles when some male language
students with shades say hello in sexy
foreign accents (Ginnie and Alice),
and I don't stare gape-mouthed when
a pretty girl in a bikini waves from a
boat (Mark and Jon).

I just stomped around wearily,
surreptitiously eating a Galaxy . . .
and then a Kit Kat . . . and a couple of
Rolos. I handed the rest round to the
family like a good generous girl. That's
another huge disadvantage of large
families. Offer your packet of Rolos
round once and they're nearly all gone
in one fell swoop.

We went to this pub garden for
lunch and I golloped down a couple
of cheese toasties and two packets of
crisps and two Cokes – all this fresh
air had made me peckish – and I had

to stoke myself up for the long trail back home along the river.

'Oh, we thought we'd go via the Green Fields,' said Graham.

I groaned. 'Graham! It's *miles*! And I've got serious blisters already.'

'I think you might like the Green Fields this particular Monday,' said Mum.

She and Graham smiled.

I didn't smile back. I *don't* like the Green Fields. They are just what their name implies. Two big green fields joined by a line of poplar trees. They don't even have a playground with swings. There isn't even an ice-cream van. There's just a lot of *grass*.

But guess what, guess what! When we got nearer the Green Fields I heard this buzz and clatter and music and laughter. And *then* I smelled wonderful mouth-watering fried onions. We turned the corner – and the Green Fields were so full you couldn't see a glimpse of grass! There was a fair there for the bank holiday.

I gave a whoop. Mark and Ginnie and Jon and Alice gave a whoop too, though they were half mocking me. Jess and Cherry gave great big whoops. Baby Rupert whooped too. He couldn't see the fair down at kneecap level in his buggy but he didn't want to be left out.

Mum and Graham smiled smugly.

Of course, the fair meant different things to all of us. Jon and Mark – *and* Graham – wanted to go straight on the dodgems. Ginnie and Alice and I went too, while Mum minded the littlies. She bought them all whippy ice creams with chocolate flakes. I wailed, saying I'd much much much sooner have an ice cream than get in a dodgem car. Mum sighed and bought me an ice cream too. But as soon as it was in my hand

I decided it *might* be fun to go on the dodgems too, so I jumped in beside Jon.

Big mistake. Mark drove straight into us, *wham-bam*, and then *splat*, the chocolate flake went right up my nostril and my ice cream went all over my face.

Mum mopped me up with one of Rupert's wet wipes, and Jon bought me another ice cream to console me. I licked this in peace while Jess and Cherry and baby Rupert sat in a kiddies' roundabout and slowly and solemnly revolved in giant teacups.

'I wonder if they've got a *proper* roundabout,' said Mum. 'I used to love those ones with the horses and the twisty gilt rails and the special music. I want to go on a real old-fashioned carousel.'

'Oh, Mum, you don't get those any more,' said Ginnie – but she was *wrong*.

We went on all sorts of *new*-fashioned rides first. We were all hurtled round and round and upside down until even I started wondering if that extra ice cream had been a good idea. Then, as we staggered queasily to the other side of the field, we heard old organ music. Mum lifted her head, listening intently.

'Is it?' she said.

It *was*. We pushed through the crowd and suddenly it was just like stepping back a hundred years. There was the most beautiful old roundabout with galloping horses with grinning mouths and flaring nostrils and scarlet saddles, some shiny black, some chocolate brown, some dappled grey. There was also one odd pink ostrich with crimson feathers and an orange beak.

'Why is that big bird there, Mum?' I asked.

'I don't know, Laura. I think they always have one odd one. Maybe it's a tradition.'

'I'm going to go on the bird,' I said.

The roundabout was slowing down. Mum had little Rupert unbuckled from his buggy so he could ride too. Graham had Cherry in his arms. Mark and Jon said the roundabout was just for kids, but when Graham asked one of them to look after Jess they both offered eagerly. Ginnie and Alice had an argument over who was going to ride on a black horse with ROBBIE on his nameplate (they both have a thing about Robbie Williams) so eventually they squeezed on together.

I rushed for the ostrich. I didn't need to. No one else wanted it. Well, *I* did. I clambered on and stroked its crimson feathers. Ostriches are definitely the odd ones out of the bird family. They can't fly. They're too heavy for their own wings.

I'm definitely the odd one out of my family – and I frequently feel too heavy for my own legs. I sat gripping the ostrich with my knees, waiting for the music to start and the roundabout to start revolving. People were still scrabbling onto the few remaining horses. A middle-aged lady in much-too-tight jeans was hauling this little toddler up onto the platform. I put out my hand to help – and then stopped, astonished. I couldn't have been more amazed if my ostrich had opened its beak and bitten me. It wasn't any old middle-aged lady bursting out of her jeans. It was Mrs Mann!

I stared at her – and she stared at me.

'Hello, Laura,' she said. 'This is my little granddaughter, Rosie.'

I made appropriate remarks to Rosie while Mrs Mann struggled to get them both up onto the ordinary brown horse beside my splendid ostrich. Mrs Mann couldn't help showing rather a lot of her vast blue-denimed bottom. I had to struggle to keep a straight face.

'Are you with your mother, Laura?' said Mrs Mann.

Oh help! Mum was in front of me with Rupert. I had written Mrs Mann that long essay about Mum and me just living together. I hadn't mentioned any babies whatsoever.

'I'm here . . . on my own,' I mumbled.

At that exact moment Mum turned round and waved at me. 'Are you all right, Laura?' she called. She nodded at Mrs Mann.

Mum and Mrs Mann looked at me, waiting for me to introduce them. I stayed silent as the music started up. *Go, go, go*, I urged inside my head. But we didn't go soon enough.

'I'm Laura's mum,' said Mum.

'I'm Laura's teacher,' said Mrs Mann. 'And this is Rosie.'

Rosie waved coyly to Rupert.

'This is my baby Rupert,' said Mum.

Mrs Mann looked surprised.

'And that's Cherry over there with my partner Graham, and Jess with my son Mark, and that's my stepson Jon, and then that's Alice and Ginnie over there, waving at those boys, the naughty girls. Sorry! We're such a big family now that it's a bit hard for anyone to take in,' said Mum, because Mrs Mann was looking so stunned.

The horses started to edge forward very very slowly, u-u-u-u-p and d-o-w-n. My tummy went up and down too as Mrs Mann looked at me.

'So you're part of a very big family, Laura?' she said.

'Yes, Mrs Mann,' I said, in a very small voice.

'Well, you do surprise me,' she said.

'Nana, Nana!' said Rosie, taking hold of Mrs Mann's nose and wiggling it backward and forward affectionately. Mrs Mann simply chuckled. I wondered how she'd react if any of our class tweaked her nose!

'We seem to be surprising each other,' shouted Mrs Mann, as the music got louder as the roundabout revved up. 'Well, Laura, judging by your long and utterly convincing autobiographical essay, you are obviously either a pathological liar – or a born writer. We'll give you the benefit of the doubt. You have the most vivid imagination of any child I've ever taught. You will obviously go far.'

And then the music was too loud for talking and the horses whirled round and round and round. I sat tight on my ostrich, and it spread its crimson wings and we flew far over the fair, all the way up and over the moon.

'**H**ey, you two. Rise and shine,' said Dad, putting his head round our bedroom door. 'It's Saturday, and we're going up to London for a special treat.'

My big sister Melissa merely grunted and burrowed further under her pink flowery duvet in the bottom bunk bed. I sat bolt upright, still wrapped like a cocoon in my *Wilma the Whale* duvet. I have a pink flowery one too, to match Melissa's, but I always kick it right off my bunk bed. I hate pink and I hate flowery. I *love* whales, especially Wilma. I don't have favourites out of all my pretend pets, but if I *did*, it would definitely be Wilma. I also have Jumper, a black and white Dalmatian dog

(Dad won him for me at a fair), Basil the boa constrictor (I made him out of Mum's old tights), Polly the Parrot (she's cardboard and getting a bit bent now), Percy the Porcupine (though he's lost his hairbrush prickles) and a whole stable of plastic ponies.

Melissa thinks I'm seriously weird having all these toy animals. Mum thinks so too. I think even Dad does. But *I* don't think I'm one bit weird. If I can't have a real pet, then pretend ones are the next best thing.

'Where are we going for our treat, Dad?' I said, disentangling Wilma so I could bounce up and down on my bunk bed.

We don't often go on days out up to London on account of the fact we haven't got much money.

'Hey, can we go to the zoo?' I asked. 'Oh, please, I want to see what a real porcupine looks like. Or perhaps we could go to the aquarium? Maybe they've got real whales?'

'You are so mad, Marty,' Melissa muttered, even though she hadn't surfaced yet. 'How could you possibly fit a whale inside an aquarium? Dad, can we go shopping? We could go along Oxford Street – or I've always wanted to go to Camden Market. Oh, please, let's go there, it would be so cool.'

'Sorry, girls. We're not going to the zoo or the aquarium or Oxford Street or Camden Market – thank goodness! We're going to a special show at Olympia.'

'A show!' we said in unison.

'Like a pop concert?' Melissa asked, poking her head out at last. 'Can we go and see Lady Gaga?'

'You're the one who's ga-ga. *I* want to see a musical, with a proper story, like *Wicked* or *The Wizard of Oz*. My friend Jaydene's been to both and she says they're brilliant,' I said.

'No concert, no musical. This is a special animal show,' said Dad.

'*Real* animals?' I gasped.

'I think so. Cats, dogs, rabbits, mice, snakes—'

'Oh, wow!' I said, hurtling down the bunk-bed ladder and dancing around in my *Spider-man* pyjamas. 'Will there be boa constrictors?'

'I doubt it. It's a show for people wanting pets. Mum and I thought it would be a good idea to take you girls and then maybe we could all agree on a good family pet.'

'Oh, double, triple wow! But Mum's always said we can't have pets because of the mess and the fuss!' I said.

'Yes, I know, but Mum's allowed to change her mind sometimes,' said Dad, grinning.

'I bet *you* changed it for her! You're the best dad in the whole world,' I said, giving him a big hug.

'Is this pet going to just be for Marty?' Melissa asked. 'Because that's not the slightest bit fair.'

'It's going to be a pet for all of us,' said Dad. 'Now, get ready, girls. Breakfast in ten minutes, OK?'

'I can't believe Mum's weakened at long long last!' I said as we got ready.

'I think it's because they're worried about you,' said Melissa, giving me a poke. 'Because you play with those tatty old toy animals all the time. They've probably consulted a child psychologist because you're so deluded.'

'Cheek! I'm not the one who's written *To my darling Melissa, I love you so much, love from Justin Bieber* all over that tatty photo you cut out of a magazine. *That's* deluded,' I said. 'Anyway, who cares *why* Mum's changed her mind? What kind of pet shall we have?'

'I think a little cat would be lovely,' said Melissa, brushing her hair. It always annoys her that her hair is brown and straight, whereas mine is blonde and curly, even though she's the girlie girl and I'm the tomboy.

'What about a *big* cat? A tiger or a leopard or a panther,' I said, leaping around the bathroom and pouncing on Melissa.

'Ow! Stop it, you idiot. No, a little cat with fluffy fur – one that will sit on my lap and purr,' said Melissa.

'You just like cute and cuddly animals. I want a really *exciting* pet,' I said.

My head felt like a Noah's Ark as animals of all shapes and sizes trumpeted and roared and whinnied in my mind. I dressed hurriedly in my comfy jeans and my *Pow!* T-shirt and my tartan Converse boots. Melissa dressed in her pink glittery heart top and her shortest skirt and her silly shoes with tiny heels. These are our favourite outfits.

Dad pretended to be dazzled by our gorgeousness when we came down for breakfast. Mum was less enthusiastic, but didn't make either of us go and change. She was in an unusually good mood.

'Can we really really really have a pet, Mum?' I asked.

'We're not making any promises. Your dad has twisted my arm about going to this Pet Show. We'll see. But I do know just how much it would mean to you, Martina – and if you had a real animal it might help you grow out of all those tatty toys you trail around.'

'See!' said Melissa. 'I was right. Mum, can we have a cat?'

'We're going to have a good look at all the pets at the Show – I just think a cat would be a very sensible choice,' said Mum. 'They're very clean and you don't have to take them for walks.'

'Couldn't we have a tiger, Mum, just a baby one, and then I could train it so it wouldn't be too fierce and would only bite people I don't like? Or what about a tarantula? *They're* fluffy, Melissa, and I'm sure it would sit on your lap,' I said.

'Try not to be silly, Martina, or I might just change my mind altogether,' said Mum.

I sometimes find it very hard *not* to be silly when I'm all excited, but I managed to keep my lips buttoned on the tube to Olympia. There were crowds and crowds all flocking into the big exhibition centre. It took ages to queue up and get inside – and then there we were, in this absolutely enormous hall, chock full of animals.

'Oh, brilliant!' I said, rushing off headlong – but Dad caught hold of me by the back of my T-shirt.

'Calm down now, Marty! Don't you *dare* go charging off like that – we'll lose you in this crowd,' he said.

'Good idea!' said Melissa, who can never resist a wise-crack. 'Let's go and see the cats!'

'We'd better do this methodically, aisle by aisle,' said Mum – but the cats happened to be on the nearest aisle.

I was all set to find them boring, simply because they were Melissa's choice – but the moment I stood in front of the first big padded cage I fell totally in love with the most beautiful Russian Blue cat called Anastasia. She wasn't really blue, just a soft grey colour, but her eyes were a bright sapphire blue. She was clearly a very special cat, because her cage was covered with red and yellow rosettes. She lay back modestly enough, her paws neatly crossed, her great blue eyes staring at me.

'Oh, I want *this* one! Oh, please, she's so beautiful!' I said. 'Can we have her?'

'Oh, yes, I love her! She's just so *cute*!' said Melissa. 'Let's have her, please!'

The lady sitting beside her cage smiled. 'Yes, she is very beautiful and very cute,' she said proudly. 'I'm afraid she's *my* cat though, and I wouldn't part with her for the world.'

'The animals here aren't for sale, girls. This is just to show you all these different pets, so you can see which sort you want,' said Dad.

'We know already, Dad! We want a Russian Blue cat!' we said.

'If you like, I'll get Anastasia out of her cage and you can stroke her,' said the lady.

'Oh, yes please!'

Melissa and I washed our hands with this special liquid and then very carefully stroked Anastasia. She stretched out luxuriously, and purred when I gently tickled under her chin.

'Could we have a cat *like* this one?' I asked.

'Well, we have another Russian Blue at home who's going to have kittens soon,' said her owner. 'You can give us your name and address if you like, and we'll put you on our waiting list.'

'Oh, WOW! Mum, Dad, can we have a Russian Blue kitten?' we begged.

'Well, maybe,' said Dad.

'Could you give us some idea how much it would cost?' said Mum.

'About five hundred,' said the lady.

Five hundred pounds for one tiny kitten! 'Maybe not,' said Dad.

'Perhaps dogs are cheaper,' I said.

We went to look at all the dogs next. We even saw a lady in a fancy costume doing a dance with her black and white collie.

'Oh, how cool! I want a dog that can dance!' I said. 'I could train it to do all sorts of tricks!'

We looked along aisle after aisle, and saw tiny lapdogs and great big butch Rottweilers and fabulous snowy white huskies.

'Oh, let's have a husky! Let's have *lots* of huskies, and then we can have a sledge and they can pull us along the road when it snows!' I said.

'We haven't even got room for one dog in the house, let alone a team of huskies,' said Mum. 'Why don't we go and look at the rabbits?'

So we cooed at the rabbits and stroked the guinea pigs and tickled the mice – but I loved the great big rats the most. Mum and Melissa went a bit squeaky themselves and backed away, but a nice man let me carry his best white rat on my shoulder. The rat peeped round at me and wriggled his little pink nose adorably.

'Oh, he's so lovely! Can we have a rat just like this one?' I begged, but sadly Mum said absolutely no way.

She was a bit strange when we got to the snake section too, but *I* thought the snakes were beautiful. I couldn't find a boa constrictor, but I held a very pretty red and white snake just like a great big living necklace.

'What does he like to eat?' I asked.

'Mice, mostly,' said the snake's owner.

'Oh dear,' I said.

'I think it's time *we* had something to eat,' said Dad.

We bought a big takeaway pizza and shared it between us.

'Well, girls, what's the verdict?' said Dad. 'What sort of pet would you like?'

'I'd like a Russian Blue cat, and a dog that can dance, and a husky, and a rabbit with floppy ears, and a guinea pig that squeaks, and a white rat that'll sit on my shoulder, and a whole cageful of mice – but I'd never ever feed them to anyone – and a vegetarian snake,' I said.

'I'd like a cat,' said Melissa. 'But they cost far too much money.'

'These are mostly special pedigree cats at this show, and they do cost a fortune,' said Dad. 'But maybe we could get an ordinary moggy from a special rescue home? I don't think a little rescue cat would cost too much money.'

'Can we have a rescue husky too, Dad? And a rescue rabbit and a rescue guinea pig and a rescue white rat and rescue mice and a rescue snake?'

'What did I say about being silly, Martina?' said Mum. But she didn't sound really cross. She was looking at Dad. 'Have you got your tube map handy? Perhaps we could go to Battersea this afternoon?'

So we went to Battersea Dogs & Cats Home. We walked round their special cattery and saw many many many cats desperate for their own special homes. Some were big and some were small, some were fierce and hissed, some cowered and looked sad. There were black cats and ginger cats and white cats and tortoise-shell cats, and we dithered in front of each one.

'I want them *all*!' I said. 'Couldn't we at least have a cat each – one for me and one for Melissa and one for Dad and one for Mum?'

'One cat for all of us!' said Mum.

And then I saw him. He was in a cage right at the end. He was much smaller than the others, just a little kitten. He was a soft grey like the Russian Blue, but he had a beautiful white face and chest and neat white paws. He had the prettiest little anxious face with a pink nose and soft white whiskers. He opened his green eyes wide and looked straight at me imploringly.

'Oh, *this* is our cat!' I said.

Melissa came and looked. 'Oh, yes! You're right, Marty! Oh, he's just so cute!'

'I love him,' said Dad.

We all looked at Mum.

'He's the sweetest little chap I've ever seen. Let's see if we can have him!' said Mum.

We had to be interviewed and

have our home checked – but now we are a family of five! Mum and Dad and Melissa and me – and our new little kitten, Tiger.

If you want to find out more about Marty and Melissa, then read Jacqueline Wilson's book

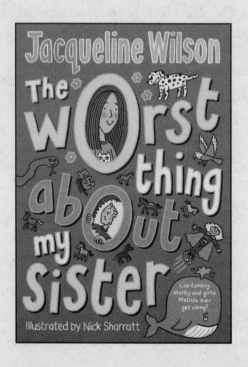

Check out the

Jacqueline Wilson

OFFICIAL WEBSITE

You'll find lots of FUN STUFF there including games, video trailers and amazing competitions. You can even customise your own page and start your own online diary!

You'll find out all about Jacqueline in her monthly diary and tour blogs, as well as seeing her replies to fan mail. You can also chat to other fans on the message board.

Join in today at
www.jacquelinewilson.co.uk

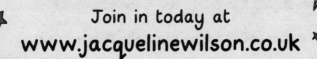

Jacqueline Wilson

Lily Alone

Sometimes Lily wishes she really was home ALONE

Illustrated by Nick Sharratt

Sometimes Lily wishes she really was home alone . . .

Jacqueline Wilson

Illustrated by Nick Sharratt

The Longest Whale Song

Can Ella's love bring Mum back?

Can Ella's love bring Mum back?

Hi! I'm Tracy. I'm ten, and I live in a Children's Home – but I'd like a real home one day, with a real family. These books are all about me. I'd read them if I were you. They're the most incredible dynamic heart-rending stories. Honest.

Meet Jacqueline Wilson's most feisty, popular and well-loved character in these three mega-bestselling books!

When Mum falls ill,
can Sadie step in
and save the day?

Will Daisy and her
special sister ever
fit in?

Lizzie doesn't want to talk to her new
step-family – so she won't say anything at all!

Perfect for fans of Jacqueline Wilson's books, now there's a pretty **2012 Diary**, a handy **Address Book** and a gorgeous **BFF Journal** to help you and your friends make the most of every single day! Packed with fun quizzes, recipes, advice, activities and fun stickers, have fun with Jacqueline all year round!

There are oodles of incredible Jacqueline Wilson
books to enjoy! Tick off the ones you have read,
so you know which ones to look for next!

- [ ] THE DINOSAUR'S PACKED LUNCH
- [ ] THE MONSTER STORY-TELLER

- [ ] THE CAT MUMMY
- [ ] LIZZIE ZIPMOUTH
- [ ] SLEEPOVERS

- [ ] BAD GIRLS
- [ ] THE BED AND BREAKFAST STAR
- [ ] BEST FRIENDS
- [ ] BIG DAY OUT
- [ ] BURIED ALIVE!
- [ ] CANDYFLOSS
- [ ] CLEAN BREAK
- [ ] CLIFFHANGER
- [ ] COOKIE
- [ ] THE DARE GAME
- [ ] THE DIAMOND GIRLS
- [ ] DOUBLE ACT
- [ ] GLUBBSLYME
- [ ] HETTY FEATHER
- [ ] THE ILLUSTRATED MUM
- [ ] JACKY DAYDREAM
- [ ] LILY ALONE
- [ ] LITTLE DARLINGS

- [ ] LOLA ROSE
- [ ] THE LONGEST WHALE SONG
- [ ] THE LOTTIE PROJECT
- [ ] MIDNIGHT
- [ ] THE MUM-MINDER
- [ ] SAPPHIRE BATTERSEA
- [ ] SECRETS
- [ ] STARRING TRACY BEAKER
- [ ] THE STORY OF TRACY BEAKER
- [ ] THE SUITCASE KID
- [ ] VICKY ANGEL
- [ ] THE WORRY WEBSITE
- [ ] THE WORST THING ABOUT MY SISTER

FOR OLDER READERS:
- [ ] DUSTBIN BABY
- [ ] GIRLS IN LOVE
- [ ] GIRLS IN TEARS
- [ ] GIRLS OUT LATE
- [ ] GIRLS UNDER PRESSURE
- [ ] KISS
- [ ] LOVE LESSONS
- [ ] MY SECRET DIARY
- [ ] MY SISTER JODIE

WORLD BOOK DAY

1 MARCH 2012

Want to **WIN**
a year's supply of **BOOKS**
for you and your school?

Of course you do…

This book is by one of our favourite authors (that's why it's in our **HALL OF FAME**!), but we want to know what *your* favourite book is (or *your* favourite character – whether it's the baddest baddie or the superest hero)!

It's that easy to win, so visit
WWW.WORLDBOOKDAY.COM now!